THE JAPANESE PILOT

A NEW BEGINNING

ROBERT EDWARD BURLEY

The Japanese Pilot
Copyright © 2020 by Robert Edward Burley

Cover Artwork by Edward Burley

Tellwell Talent
www.tellwell.ca

ISBN
978-0-2288-3059-7 (Paperback)
978-0-2288-3060-3 (eBook)

THE JAPANESE PILOT

The Winnebago pulled up beside the fuel pumps at the service station halfway between Greenvale and Rockhampton. The sign read, "Halfway Service Centre - Shinzo Watanabe, Proprietor."

The tourists stepped out of their vehicle and stretched their legs in the red dust.

"Hey Mate," said the tourist, "have you any amenities?"

"They're around the back of the restaurant. You should find they're unlocked," I said.

"Fill her up with diesel please," he called as he turned to walk around the corner.

I opened the tank and soon had the diesel flowing.

A woman, apparently his partner, climbed out of the vehicle followed by two young children of about nine or ten.

"Are there any amenities?" she enquired.

"Yes madam, they're around behind the restaurant," I answered.

When they'd all used the amenities, they went into the restaurant, a friendly lady came and greeted them with a smile.

"Order something and I will cook it up for you," she said, handing them menus.

She soon had the grill sizzling, cooking up four burgers. I washed my hands and put on a fresh white apron and started mixing four milkshakes.

When the guests had finished their meal, they ordered coffee. "Gerty makes the best coffee in Northern Queensland!" I informed them.

When they'd eaten enough the children went out to play in the back yard.

I poured himself a mug of coffee and sat down to talk with them.

"Have you travelled far?" I asked, taking a sip of the coffee.

"We've come from Brisbane. We left Rocky yesterday and we've been driving all day today.

By the way, "I'm Peter Davis and this is my wife Jennifer. I'm curious, how did a man of Japanese nationality, come to be the proprietor of a roadhouse halfway between Rockhampton and Greenvale," he asked.

"If you'd like another cup of coffee, I'll tell you all about it. You'll be surprised." I said.

"In January 1942, I sat in a zero on the flight deck an aircraft carrier, the Honshu Maru, revving my powerful engine, in preparation to fly on a mission to bomb Darwin. Yes, I was a Japanese pilot. I remember how noisy it was. There were other planes lining up, waiting for the signal to be launched from the carrier. I was very nervous waiting to take off as I thought I might not make it back alive.

Adrenalin was surging through me as I sat there strapped in and ready. It was so noisy I could only hear the drone of the engines. I pulled my flying goggles down over my eyes and braced myself. Then the moment I had been anticipating arrived.

"Go!" signalled the ground crewman as he dropped his flag.

My aeroplane was catapulted from the deck and into the air in one motion and I flew up into a holding pattern, circling around the Honshu Maru. When we were all airborne our squadron leader led us off to the south-west, towards our target, Australia.

I had a full load of bombs to release onto the city of Darwin. As we arrived, it was already aflame from the earlier strikes. Anti-aircraft flak from the ground was popping and exploding all around me and my plane shook from the close percussion. I was anxious and sweating so my goggles kept fogging up so that I couldn't see clearly. I was lucky not to have been hit. I saw one of my fellow pilots hit by flak. His zero exploded and he was killed. I continued and reached my target near the harbour. I aimed carefully and released the bombs, but from what I could see they exploded in the water next to the wharves. I felt great disappointment for having failed my mission.

I turned to fly back to my carrier the Honshu Maru in the Timor Sea in the north but suddenly my zero was struck by anti-aircraft fire and the engine was billowing smoke. I changed course and headed south-east into Northern Queensland. All I could see below was broad expanse of trees and plains. There were no signs of settlements or people. If I managed to bring the wounded zero down, I would be stranded in the Australian bush.

Fortunately, I was able to keep the plane aloft for what seemed like ages but when the engine began to stall, I lost all control of it and it swung dangerously from side to side. I'd had plenty of training flying aeroplanes, but no experience crash landing them. I realised that the consequences could be serious, perhaps fatal.

My mind was racing, thinking of what I could do. But a huge explosion as my engine blew up decided my response. I pulled at my canopy release handle and found that it was jammed. The flames and black smoke obscured my vision and the cockpit was getting uncomfortably hot from the engine fire, but I continued to struggle with the canopy release latch.

I reached down beside my leg and found a wrench and belted the latch in a frenzy.

As the flames lapped over the front of the plane, I broke the latch and the canopy flew back and ripped off. I climbed up quickly and jumped out of the plane just it time. As I drifted down swinging in my parachute, I saw the plane hit the ground far below me and explode in a bright flame and a huge plume of black smoke.

As I glided down, I noticed the sparse bush and was fortunate to land in a clear patch avoiding the trees. I hit the ground hard and felt the pain as my ankle buckled under me. I tried to stand up, but my ankle hurt so badly that I had to remain where I was for the time being. It was a very hot day and it was deadly quiet. There weren't even birds calling apart from a distant caw from a black crow. I lay back in my parachute and covered my head from the harsh sunshine that was beating down on me.

I peeked out with one eye and noticed a big lizard with a flicking tongue come wandering out of the bush towards me. I don't know if I was more startled or afraid. He was about a metre long, mainly black, with yellow stripes on his body. I thought that he might have been a baby dragon and reached for my knife to fight him off, but he hissed at me, turned, and waddled back into the bush.

Not long after the lizard's visit, I saw a kangaroo come hopping nearby. I had only seen pictures of them in books. This was the first time I'd seen a real one. I was amazed at how it moved. It appeared to be a beautiful, docile creature

I thought to myself, "There certainly are some weird animals in Australia."

As I lay there the relentless sun beat down on me so I did the only thing I could do, I crawled under the shade of a big tree. I had a ration fruit bar in my flight suit pocket so I tried to eat it, but my mouth was so dry I couldn't swallow it. I was very thirsty and realised that if I didn't get something to drink, I would die out here on my own of dehydration.

A bit later on I heard the sound of an engine coming up the road towards me. It was a local farmer driving a tractor and wagon up the road. Later I learned that he was Trevor Flanagan.

Trevor summed up the situation very quickly. He pulled up his tractor and wagon, put on the handbrake and walked over to me.

"G'day Mate!" he said, "Did you get shot down?"

He was my enemy so I drew my knife and dived at him, yelling, "Kill! Kill!"

He avoided my attack easily and stood his ground. He said, "That little pocket-knife wouldn't cut through my singlet."

In a flash he took the pocket-knife from me, folded it up, and handed it back to me.

He said, "Keep that to peel your oranges Mate," and grinned a wide grin.

When he realised that I couldn't walk, he picked me up bodily and put me onto the wagon and said, "I'll take you home to Dad, he'll know what to do with you."

Before we went, he raised a big water bag, opened it and let the water pour into his mouth. He passed the water bag to me and said, "Have a drink. But go easy Mate."

The sweet, cool water was wonderful as I was very thirsty. I was extremely grateful to the farmer. As I felt life surge back into me. I nodded my thanks.

Although the farmer put down seed bags on the tray of the trailer the ride was very rough and uncomfortable, and I had to hang on all the way in case I fell off. My ankle was causing me great discomfort. Above the sound of the tractor engine

I could hear the farmer singing. It just seemed so strange to me. I was finding that lots of Australian things were seeming strange to me.

Sometime later we arrived at the farm. It seemed to be organised and homely with fences and gardens in good order. The farmer, Trevor, parked the tractor and wagon and helped me into the house. I had to limp all the way.

A man, I learnt later was Col Flanagan, was sitting at the kitchen table when we came in. He was a man of about sixty-five years of age. He had lines on his face from many years working in the sun. He was very brown. He had intelligent eyes and a pleasant, content attitude. He looked at me and asked, "Who's this bloke Trevor?"

"I came across him when I was coming home from the paddock. His plane crashed and he parachuted to safety. He hurt his ankle when he landed," said Trevor.

"You poor fellow," said Mrs Flanagan. "Does your ankle hurt?" she asked.

I couldn't understand what she was saying, but I could understand that she was being kind to me. She got me to roll up my flight suit leg and examined my ankle.

She touched it and I winced, so she brought in a big tin dish and gently soaked my ankle in warm water, washed it and bandaged it with a support bandage. It began to feel a bit better. I smiled at her for helping me. She smiled a kindly smile back to me.

Mrs Flanagan, Beth, was younger than Col but time had not erased her original natural beauty. She was a pleasant woman of about fifty-five. Her hair was greying but it suited in the style she wore it. She had kind, lovely blue eyes and was quick to flash a smile.

My English at that time was about as good as Col's Japanese.

Col pointed to himself and said, "My name's Col Flanagan, what's your name Mate?"

"Me Col," he said pointing at himself, "Col." I understood.

I said, "Me, Shinzo Watanabe!"

"How did you come here Shinzo?" asked Col.

I couldn't understand what he was saying but I stood up and made actions with my hands to show that I had been flying my plane then being hit by ground fire and my plane crashing and exploding. I pretended that I was parachuting down to the ground.

At this point Mrs Flanagan called everyone to the table, me as well.

Col showed me to the bathroom and washed his hands, so I washed mine as well and dried them on a towel Col handed me. When I sat down at the table, we all joined hands and they said what seemed to be a blessing over the food with their heads bowed. I bowed my head in respect to their customs.

I was confused by their eating utensils. There seemed to be knives, forks and spoons everywhere. I had only ever used one pair of chop-sticks.

I managed a spoon quite well when Mrs Flanagan brought out a big plate of steaming vegetables and roast meat and white sauce.

I was starving but refrained to show respect. Col showed me how to cut the meat into smaller pieces to eat with a sharp knife and a fork. He was very patient with me.

I did well with the meat and vegetables but had trouble with the peas and chased them on the table. This made my hosts smile.

Trevor was seated opposite me, Col sat at the head of the table and Beth sat at the opposite end. When Col asked me if I liked the food, I smiled at him and said, "Yes!" nodding my head to indicate yes. When I spoke in English everybody smiled.

Col asked Trevor if he'd planted seeds in the far paddock.

Trevor nodded and said, "Yeah Dad. But it's bloody dry out there. We'll have to get that pump going to get some water to irrigate."

"Well tomorrow you take Shinzo, if he can walk, to help you with the pipes and we'll soon get some water flowing," said Col.

Mrs Flanagan showed me to a comfortable room with a lovely soft bed. I removed my pilot's uniform and slept in my service underwear. Before she left, she showed me a chamber pot in case I needed to pee during the night. I couldn't stop from laughing as she demonstrated how a man would use the pot. When I stopped laughing, I got into bed. Beth poked her head around the door and said, "Goodnight Shinzo. Tomorrow we'll be getting up at 5.00 am, so sleep well!"

I said to myself, 05.00, and set the alarm on my watch, and thought, "these Australians are very kind. But still they are my enemy, I must try to get back to Japan."

I could hear Col and Beth softly talking together as I drifted off to sleep, "Shouldn't we be notifying someone about this Japanese pilot Col?" asked Beth.

"I suppose we should, but let's give him a few days to see what he's like. He seems pretty harmless," said Col.

Over a big hot breakfast of bacon, eggs and buttered toast, Col, Trevor and I sat around the kitchen table drinking hot tea.

By six o'clock we were loaded and ready to go out to the paddocks.

Beth handed me a big package of sandwiches and a thermos flask of tea. I smiled at her and said, "Arigato – thank you."

Beth smiled back and said, "Have a good day."

Trevor was a quiet fellow not inclined to say much, so I sat on the back of the truck watching the strange Australian animals. Down by a little waterhole I saw a group of five of the strangest birds I'd ever seen. They were taller than a man and had no wings. They had feathers around their lower body and very long necks. They had big alert eyes and could run very fast.

I called to Trevor, "See, see," pointing at the birds.

"Emu," said Trevor, "Can run fast, but cannot fly."

I repeated, "Emu!"

On the side of the waterhole lay a very long crocodile lying, sunning himself on the sand.

"Croc has many teeth," chomping his own teeth to demonstrate, "Stay away Shinzo he bites!" Trevor said waving his hand from side to side."

I mimicked him, "Crock, stay away Shinzo. He bites!"

"That's right Shinzo," said Trevor, smiling at me.

We arrived at the far paddock after ten.

Trevor said to me, "Cup of tea and a sandwich first," opening the sandwiches.

Trevor poured us both a cup of tea into metal mugs and handed me a beef sandwich with homemade pickles. We sat on the back of the truck eating. I wore a broad brimmed hat that Trevor had given me called an 'Akubra,' to protect me from the sun. I wore my pilot's trousers and a cotton shirt Beth gave me. Trevor wore an 'Akubra' too and kept his shirt sleeves rolled down to prevent sunburn.

When we'd finished our morning tea, Trevor cleaned up and put the remaining sandwiches and the thermos in the truck, then did something I didn't understand. He raised his leg, like a Sumo wrestler, and passed wind loudly, "That was a good feed Mate!" he said.

I tried to do the same as Trevor. I lifted my leg and said, "That was a good feed mate, but I only produced a fizzer."

Trevor smiled and said, "You'll get the hang of it Mate."

Trevor gave me a friendly slap on the shoulder and we both walked off laughing.

In the old corrugated iron pumphouse Trevor tipped in the fresh fuel I had helped him carry from the truck and set about priming the engine. Then he gave the crank a mighty pull.

The ancient rusty engine went "burble, burble," then shuddered to a halt.

I said, "I fix Trevor."

Trevor was surprised to hear me speak English.

I pointed to the shifting wrench and Trevor handed it to me. I loosened the six little housing bolts and opened the carburettor housing. Then I used a screwdriver to unscrew a little filter valve. I lifted it out. A little dab of greasy dirt fell out. Then I placed the valve, replaced the cover and tightened the six housing bolts.

Trevor primed the engine and I said, "You try."

The engine went, "burble, burble," and continued to burble. It was running beautifully.

Trevor grabbed me and started to dance. He said, "You Beauty Shinzo you got it going!"

I was happy too and said, "You Beauty Trevor."

Water began to gush up through the bore and began spraying into the empty dam. It was hot artesian water, but it would cool down soon above the ground. Then we could send it along the long irrigation pipes and drains to reach the newly planted wheat crops.

I felt very happy watching the pump doing its job knowing that I had something to do with getting it going. I had always enjoyed tinkering with engines.

"Shinzo you are very good with engines," said Trevor.

I guessed what he was saying and replied, "Arigato."

Trevor assumed I was saying, 'thank you', which I was.

We shook hands. We spent the afternoon laying irrigation pipes and directing the water to the crops. It had cooled by this time. My ankle was sore, but the pain was tolerable.

At four o'clock we stopped work and had a cup of tea from the thermos flask and ate the remainder of the sandwiches.

We were satisfied with the work we'd done. The dam was already about a third full. Trevor said we would leave the pump running overnight and come back the following day to check the engine.

We packed up the tools and sat together in the cab for the long drive home.

As we drove along Trevor sang 'Waltzing Matilda'. I listened with interest and soon began to hum along.

When he finished, I clapped him and asked, "Trevor. What is a 'jumbuck'?"

He said, "A 'jumbuck is a bloody sheep," and did a sheep call, "Bah-ah-ah, bah-ah-ah."

I caught on, "a 'jumbuck' is a bloody sheep. Bah-ah-ah, bah-ah-ah."

We both laughed at my sheep imitation.

We arrived just after sunset, put the tools in the shed and washed up for the evening meal.

Mrs Flanagan had cooked up a roast leg of lamb and vegetables. I combed my hair and changed my shirt before I came to the table.

Col and Trevor talked about the old artesian pump and how I got it to start by cleaning the carburettor valve. Col was impressed and to said me, "Shinzo you did very well," and smiled.

I said, "Arigato Col." I was very happy. I regarded Col as the Father of the house and showed him the respect he deserved.

Talk around the table was happy and 'Beth,' Mrs Flanagan, told Col she wanted new curtains in the loungeroom. He agreed to buy the material she'd selected the next time they went to Greenvale in a few weeks' time.

Trevor told Col he'd need some new leather work-boots and shirts while they were in town.

Col said, "We'll get some workpants and boots for Shinzo too. I'll bank some wages for him at the bank. Would you like that Shinzo?"

I only guessed at what Col was saying, but when he pulled out a pound note, I smiled and said, "Arigato. Thankyou Mr Col."

"Just Col," he replied.

"Arigato Just Col," I said, not understanding.

"It's going to take a bit of time," said Col smiling.

Trevor and I worked well together fencing, feeding stock and irrigating crops. Trevor taught me the skills that I would need to be a good farmer.

One day Trevor was tying off a strain of barbed wire when suddenly, a black snake bit him on the calf muscle. He was wearing short pants, so the bite went deep into his flesh.

Trevor yelled out, "Shinzo, Quick! Help me Mate! I've been bitten by a snake!"

I reacted instinctively and cut the snake's head off and prised it from Trevor's leg. Trevor was rolling around in pain holding his leg. I took off my leather belt and made a tourniquet and applied it above his knee. Trevor was sweating heavily.

"Help me to the vehicle Shinzo. Take me home to Beth," he said.

I assisted him up into the cab and he said, "Drive Shinzo, drive!"

I jumped into the driver's seat, started the engine and drove quickly in the direction of the homestead as if I'd been driving all my life.

As I drove along the bumpy bush track, I kept looking over at Trevor. He was in a good deal of pain and wincing at every bump. I was very worried that Trevor might die

I remember when I first met Trevor, I had run at him with a little knife trying to kill him. Now here I was almost breaking my neck to get him to help so that we could save his life.

It took us about forty-five minutes to get to the homestead. We'd made good time. I sounded the horn all the way up to the house. Beth, who had been doing the ironing, came running out to find out what all the noise was about.

I answered in my broken English, "Snake bite Trevor on leg!"

Beth knew what to do so I helped her to get him into the loungeroom. Beth released the tourniquet and washed the bite site with antiseptic solution. She dried the limb and bandaged it from thigh to ankle. Trevor was still conscious but was starting to get very groggy.

Col came in from ploughing and asked what had happened,

He looked very worried when he found out and asked, "Shinzo what colour was the snake?"

"Was he black or brown?"

I was confused with the English words. Suddenly it came to me,

"Snake was 'black' Col." "Black!"

He said, "That's okay. The poison from a black snake is not as bad as venom from a brown snake.

"He be okay?" I asked.

"I'll take him to Greenvale hospital for help," said Col, "Shinzo you look after Beth and the farm okay!"

I said, "Yes Col me look after."

I refuelled the vehicle and we helped get Trevor into the cab and they took off for Greenvale hospital sending gravel flying.

When they arrived at the hospital the doctor went into action immediately infusing antivenom and monitoring Trevor's vital signs. By seven thirty that night Trevor's fever was beginning to abate and he was starting to speak coherently. We were very worried about Trevor and when Col phoned from the hospital and told us he was awake and responding to treatment we were greatly relieved.

"You're lucky Trevor. You got quite a enormous injection of venom from that bite," said the doctor. Your Dad got you here just in time,"

Trevor rested throughout the night and was feeling much stronger in the morning. By noon following day, two days after the bite, they were able to undertake the long journey home.

Col stopped at the Greenvale store and picked up a few extra groceries we needed. He also bought a dozen bottles of beer.

Col said to me, "Shinzo you saved his life. He couldn't have driven himself home."

I said to Col, "Mr Col you take Trevor to Greenvale. You save him too."

Col knocked off the bottle top and poured us both a glass of beer. He made Beth a 'shandy', beer mixed fifty-fifty with lemonade.

We clinked our glasses together and said, "Cheers!"

I said, "Cheers Col and Beth."

I drank my glass of beer and said, "Very good!"

"Today might have ended very differently. We could have lost Trevor. It was a good thing Shinzo knew how to make a tourniquet and how to drive the lorry."

I said to Col, "Trevor teach me to drive."

Col and I sat by the fire after Beth had gone off to bed.

"Col," I asked.

"Mate what is it?" he asked.

"Am I a coward. Should I commit 'hari kiri' because I failed?" I asked.

Col thought for a minute and then spoke,

"If you kill yourself you won't change anything. The War will still go on until it finishes. We can't change anything. You have your whole life ahead of you. You are becoming a good farmer. One day you will have a family of your own, perhaps, your own property."

"The things you say are true. But I swore to serve the Emperor. I swore I'd die for him," I mentioned.

He said, "Shinzo we swear allegiance to our King, but he will never meet us or know that we exist. We can live, die, and be washed away in time and he will never know anything about us. You are more useful to the world alive. Casualties in this War are already enormous, in the millions. Would your body being thrown onto the sacrificial fire be of any benefit? No. War is not glorious, it is a tragedy. So many people being blown to pieces and machine gunned. For what? Nobody wins. Women, children, animals, young and old are caught up in it and killed, starved or displaced. Those of us, here alive, must stay alive and rebuild the world after the War. Good people like you and me need to grow the food for the survivors. Don't throw all this away. I don't know why you were shot down and came here but I believe it is your destiny, and your opportunity, to make a new beginning."

I thought about what Col had said and commented, "You're right Col. We must survive to build a better future. And one more thing," I said.

"What's that?" he asked.

"I like Beth's cooking," I said.

"You're right. I will not 'hari kiri'. I work hard Col and do my best."

Col said, "We have a saying here and it goes like this, 'I wouldn't be dead for quids.' Basically, it means, being alive is much better than being dead, wouldn't you agree?

"Thanks Col. I'm okay. I think I'll go to bed now. Goodnight," I said.

"Goodnight Mate," said Col.

The next morning Trevor was feeling a bit hungover but improving. He ate a hearty breakfast and told Col and Beth what had happened the day he'd been bitten. Then I brought in a seed bag and tipped out the contents. The snake's head rolled out onto the floor. I had put it into the bag and thrown it into the back of the truck the day it had bitten Trevor.

It was a big black snake, with a very wide head with long sharp fangs.

"Gee Trevor you're lucky to survive a bite from that big bloke," said Col.

"Oh well you've got an interesting souvenir," said Beth.

She put the snake's head into a jar with methylated spirits to preserve it and gave it to Trevor.

"There son, the snake that nearly killed you!" said Beth.

Life resumed its usual pattern on the homestead and one night after tea Col spoke to me at the kitchen table.

"You've been here six months now. I've been putting two pounds into the bank for you for your work here on the farm. You now have a total of one hundred and eighty pounds in the bank. What do you think?" he asked.

I answered, "Very happy Col. You help Shinzo very much, Arigato Col," I bowed, smiling.

Col asked, "Is there anything you'd like me to buy for you in town?"

I considered his offer and said, "Yes you please take twenty pounds and buy a nice new dress for Mrs Flanagan, I am grateful she feeds me very well."

He replied, "That's a lovely thought Shinzo. What coloured dress would you want me to buy?"

I told him, "She likes blue with white flowers. I was looking in a book with her and she pointed it out to me. I show you."

I went and got the catalogue and showed him.

"See Col, she likes this one," I indicated.

"Okay Mate. I'll order it for you, but I'd like you to give it to her. Her birthday is in five weeks. With any luck it'll be back just in time," he said.

"Shinzo you're a good man. I'm glad you didn't bomb us," he said.

Col turned to go, but I called him.

"Col," I said.

"Yes Mate?" he asked.

I said, "You are a good man too."

Col winked and nodded and went off to his room to be with Beth.

Harvest came around. It was a very busy time on the farm. Trevor taught me to drive the tractor and I gradually learnt to operate it. I also drove the combine harvester through the fields of waving golden wheat and soon the holding bins were overflowing. I felt a great sense of satisfaction harvesting the wheat and loading into the big bins.

"What we do now Trevor the bins are full?" I asked

He knew the answer, he usually did, "We'll put it in the big silo then the truck can come and collect it and drive it to the mills," he replied.

Trevor never minded answering my questions because he knew I would remember the answers and help him when there was something to be done.

One morning the whole house was awakened by the loud sounding of a truck horn. Col looked out the window to see who it was.

"It's Dave Robinson, the delivery driver. We'll have to get Shinzo out of sight until he goes. He'll probably be here all day," he said to Beth.

Col knocked on my door and said, "Listen carefully. Take the truck and go to the north paddock. There's someone here with supplies but he might report you to the police. Do you understand? Take some food and go out the back way. But you'll have to hurry. Come back tonight. I'll keep him talking out the front. Good luck Mate."

"Thanks Col," I called. I jumped up, grabbed my boots, dressed and was away in minutes. While Col was speaking with the visitor he heard me start up and drive away, I would be okay.

"G'day Dave how are you going?" asked Col.

"G'day Col. I'm doing okay Mate," he answered.

"I've got a surprise for you," said Dave.

From the other side of his truck jumped Gerty, Col's niece.

"I'll be blowed, Gerty! We haven't seen you for ages. You were just a little girl when I saw you in Brisbane. Now you're all grown up. What brings you to our lovely homestead?" he asked.

Throwing her arms around his neck and kissing him on the cheek she said,

"Oh, Uncle Col it's so wonderful to see you. Mum has sent me to stay with you until the War's over. Relatives have crowded into our house and taken over my room. Please can I stay with you, pretty please?" she asked.

"Gerty you're always welcome with me and Aunty Beth. I'll help you bring your things in and Aunty Beth can fill you in on all the gossip," he said.

Dave and Col unloaded the supplies into the shed and soon Trevor, awoken by the noise, came out to help.

"Trevor, Gerty's here to stay with us. She's inside talking to Beth," said Col.

"Oh!" said Trevor rising his eyebrows, "That's interesting," wondering how they were going to explain Shinzo to Gerty.

"Come in Dave," invited Col, "Beth's got some breakfast on for us."

"You don't have to ask me twice Mate. I know how well she cooks," said Dave.

As they came in, they washed their hands and sat at the big breakfast table. Trevor and Gerty came in. Gerty immediately put on an apron and assisted Beth. She served them fried eggs, bacon and sausage, fried tomato, baked beans and hot buttered toast. Gerty poured them all a nice hot cup of tea.

Beth and Gerty sat down and joined in heartily and they all enjoyed breakfast together.

Col opened the conversation and asked, "What's the news in Rocky Dave?"

"Well Col, everybody's worried about the War. Most of Europe and North Africa is under the control of Hitler and Mussolini and the Japanese are making their way down through New Guinea. Everyone is concerned that Australia will be next.

Thankfully since the bombing of Pearl Harbour, the Americans are in on our side and the Aussies in Africa have been brought back to fight in New Guinea to defend Australia. Our Prime Minister, John Curtain, says that he wants Aussie troops to defend Australia first. Some very heavy fighting is going on in New Guinea and the Pacific islands.

The Allied Forces in the Pacific are under the command of General Douglas MacArthur.

Beef prices are good, lamb even better and wheat prices are well up, so you should bring in a good dividend at the end of the year," said Dave.

"More toast?" asked Beth.

"Yes please, Beth, just one piece please," said Dave.

"But how are the ordinary people handling it?" asked Col.

"They're talking about nothing else. Some people are building concrete or galvanised iron bomb shelters in their backyards in case of bomb attacks.

There was news in the paper that a mini-submarine shelled Newcastle trying to hit the BHP, but guns at Fort Scratchley chased it away. A similar submarine fired a torpedo in Sydney Harbour killing sailors sleeping upon the ship 'Kuttabul'. Good news though, the mini-submarine was depth charged and blown up killing the crew."

"Oh well," said Col, "Let's pray that we can beat them off."

Dave gave Col the invoice and he signed it.

"Thank you for the wonderful breakfast Beth. Can I leave a pound for you?" said Dave.

"Dave you drive all this way to help us, how could we charge an old friend like you for breakfast. You are our guest."

"Thank you Beth I appreciate that," said Dave.

"Well if you don't mind, I'll get going. I must get over to Beralla to deliver their supplies.

Again, thank you for the breakfast. I'll see you in about three months. Cheerio!" said Dave. He shook hands with Col and

Trevor, then climbed into his big truck, started it up and drove off with dust flying and squawking chooks cackling after him.

Beth invited Gerty to sit and have a talk in the loungeroom. Trevor came in and sat down with them.

"Aunty Beth you look so serious. Is everything alright?" said Gerty picking up on their mood.

"Gerty, we've got something discuss but we don't want you to mention it to anyone else," said Beth.

"One day while driving home Trevor saw a plane going down in flames and came across the pilot who'd parachuted down. Trevor went over to him and assisted him because he'd sprained his ankle. The pilot was Japanese," said Col.

"Oh," said Gerty, "Did Trevor kill him?"

"Oh no," said Col.

"The pilot, Shinzo, has almost become one of the family. He eats with us, works with us and sleeps in our house. He's an intelligent, helpful young fellow. Recently, when Trevor was bitten by a black snake, Shinzo saved Trevor's life by applying a tourniquet and driving him here so we could get him to Greenvale hospital to receive the anti-venom," Col said.

"Look," said Gerty getting heated, "This Jap might be a great bloke to you, but you're forgetting that he's our enemy. If we are found hiding him, we could all be sent to prison."

"He didn't start the War. They told him that if he didn't attack Darwin, he would be executed, and his family would be sent to a concentration camp. What choice did he have?" said Col.

"I'll tell you what Gerty. We'll introduce you to Shinzo and you can meet him.

If you still believe we need to hand him in authorities, we will give you the option of making the phone call," said Col.

"Okay but you would probably hate me and ask me to leave too," she replied.

"Gerty, Shinzo is like one of us, family almost, and you want to kick him out. I really think you should meet him first, before you form any impressions," said Col.

During the supply man's visit I drove out to the paddock and found a big shady tree to park beneath. Many thoughts were running through my head as I sat waiting in the truck. What if the supply man had seen me drive away and make a report? Col, Beth and Trevor would get into serious trouble, perhaps sent to prison. I hadn't realised that by helping me they had placed themselves in a very difficult predicament.

Being alone all day gave me time to reflect about the time I had spent in Australia and remember all the kindness that Col and Beth had shown me. Since I'd landed the Flanagans had shown me nothing but consideration. They'd included me in their lives and treated me as a human being, not as their enemy.

I finally decided that leaving them and making my way to the coast was my only alternative. I knew I would miss them, but I didn't want to get any of them into trouble.

I resolved to discuss it with Col when I arrived home.

As sat and watched the sun going down. I couldn't get over the size of this beautiful land and its wonderful colours. As the sun reached the horizon the land appeared to turn a deep red. The surrounding plains turned a purple hue. I compared this place to where I had come from, an ancient green land with great tracts of houses filled with millions of people.

I had never dreamt that there were places like this with broad expanses of land and wonderful animals. I began to think why this twist of fate had happened to me.

When I guessed that the supply man had gone, I started my engine and headed back to the homestead.

At eight o'clock I parked the truck, in the big shed, washed up and came in for dinner. Everything was very quiet. I hoped all was well.

As I came into the kitchen I and looked up and saw a lovely young woman sitting at the kitchen table. From the very first time I saw her I was smitten.

She was about my age, with reddish blonde hair and had a serious expression on her face as if she ruled the world. She looked at me then flashed a scornful look.

Col broke the silence and said, "Gerty, this is our friend 'Shinzo Watanabe'. Shinzo this is our niece, 'Gerty Williamson.'"

"Hello Gerty. I am Shinzo," I said, bowing as was my custom.

I noticed that she was blushing. She was so beautiful. I smiled at her and, reluctantly, she returned it.

Beth served the meal and we all joined hands and said the blessing. Gerty held my hand and I felt the electricity between us.

We began our meal and soon conversation was centred around Dave's visit and Gerty's trip.

Gerty was very forward, and not restrain herself. She came directly to the point,

"Shinzo why are Japanese soldiers attacking my country?" she asked.

"I didn't want to attack Australians. It was my government that decided to attack Australia. I was ordered to attack, or I would be executed. In my place Gerty, what would have you done?"

The question stumped her. She thought about it and said, "I suppose I would have done what you did. But don't you ever try to hurt Beth, Col or Trevor," she said with a warning expression.

"Why would I hurt them? They are very kind to me. They treat me like one of their own," I told her.

"Well you make sure you don't take advantage of their kindness or you'll have me to deal with Mr Watanabe," she threatened.

"I'd never do that Gerty," I said.

When Beth served the dessert of bread and butter custard, she whispered to Gerty,

"Well. Do you still want to turn him in?"

She said, "He is very nice I must admit."

I smiled at Gerty and winked, just like Col winks.

Gerty was very good playing the piano, so when we'd washed up and packed away the dishes, we sat around in the loungeroom and listened to her play some familiar songs.

I surprised everyone when I burst into song when Gerty's played 'Waltzing Matilda."

"Where did you learn that? "asked Col.

"We sing it in the truck all the time Dad, when we're on our way out to the paddocks or on our way home," said Trevor.

When the music stopped Col asked me, "Shinzo do you know what a 'jumbuck' is?"

"A 'jumbuck' is a bloody sheep. Trevor told me so," I said.

"'A 'sheep', not a 'bloody sheep,'" said Col

They all laughed at this.

As time went by Gerty got to know and like me and I got to know and like her too.

On Sundays I'd take Gerty for a drive up to the dam. Sometimes we watched the wild ducks out on the dam. It a was nice place with overhanging weeping willows and native flowering bushes and ferns all around us. It was a natural wonderland and rapidly became our favourite place to visit. But most of all it had something that we could never have at the farm, privacy. We made the most of it.

We often took a picnic hamper in the truck and put down a blanket and enjoyed a picnic lunch. Before we laid the blanket, I always took a solid stick and hit the grass all around to make sure that there were no snakes. After Trevor's encounter with the snake I wasn't taking any chances.

We spent many happy hours together by the dam, talking, laughing, and cuddling. One day I leaned over and kissed Gerty for the very first time. It was the most wonderful moment in my life. Gerty was so beautiful I wanted to spend the rest of my life with her. We had both fallen in love. The more we saw of each other, the stronger our feelings grew. Wherever we went, we held hands. When we listened to the radio, I put my arm around her and she put her head on my shoulder.

I remember fondly those happy days, driving home with my arm around her and the scent of her lovely hair. Gerty was my first and my only love.

Eventually I realised that I must do something. One night I spoke to Col and explained what was happening.

"Col, I fall in love with Gerty and she fall in love with me. What can we do?" I asked.

"Well Mate if she loves you and you love her why don't you ask her to marry you?" he advised.

"But what about church and celebrations and all that?" I asked.

"Don't worry about all that, it's mainly for show and we don't have a lot of relatives to invite. Gerty's parents have passed away long ago, and I doubt if your family will be coming over to Australia for a wedding," said Col.

"We can arrange for you to get married in the Registry Office in Greenvale. We will tell them that you are Chinese, they won't know the difference. But we must use your real name. Would you like to take a chance?" he asked me. "You can write your name in Japanese, and they won't know if its Chinese or Japanese."

"I will ask Gerty. But what do I have to do?" I asked him.

"It's pretty easy Mate. Just kneel down on one knee and say "'Gerty I love you, will you marry me?" he advised.

The following Saturday I took Gerty for a drive out to the dam and parked under our shady tree.

I was tongue tied at first, thinking in both Japanese and English at the same time. But I followed Col's instructions, and went down on one knee, my heart thumping and said, "Darling Gerty. I love you. Will you marry me?"

She began to cry, but, as she explained, it was with happiness.

"Oh yes Shinzo, I would love to marry you," she answered.

I felt my heart leap with joy. I was going to marry my beautiful Gerty.

I stood up and kissed her and we embraced in the truck under that old willow tree.

She felt so warm and wonderful in my arms. I had never been in love before. I'd never even had a girlfriend until I met Gerty.

I placed the ring on her finger Beth had handed me on the way out. She said it was her left to her by her mother. It was a good fit.

Gerty smiled and held it up to watch the sun shining through it. It sparkled as only real diamonds do.

When we arrived back at the homestead Gerty ran to Col and Beth to tell them our news.

They offered us their congratulations and Beth kissed us both on the cheek and Col shook my hand.

When Trevor came in and heard the news, he shook my hand and said, "You beauty Shinzo you and I are going to be brothers-in-law."

"You beauty Trevor, now we will be brothers," I said.

"That's lovely Gert. We can have a celebration here at the homestead. We can both cook for it," Beth said enthusiastically.

Col and I sat together and worked out the details and decided on a plan over a hot cup of tea. Gerty and Beth worked out their details in the loungeroom.

Beth and Gerty concentrated on making the wedding dress and after a few weeks, it was finished. It was perfect. Gerty was very pleased with it.

Beth decided to wear the dress Shinzo had bought for her by mail. When she tried it on to see if it still fitted. Gerty told her,

"You look gorgeous, Aunty Beth." She spun around like a model and she looked much younger than her age.

Col drove to Greenvale to make an appointment to meet the Registrar and arrange for the names on the certificate. He was lucky to get one that afternoon.

He also paid a fee of five pounds to the clerk, Mr Branigan, for the duties.

The date was set for Saturday the seventeenth of August. Time was passing so quickly but by the sixteenth they had everything ready.

The night before the ceremony, Col, Trevor and I sat in the loungeroom talking about the future and drinking some beer.

Col said, "Shinzo, when you and Gerty are married you will have to live somewhere. Of course, you are both welcome to live here indefinitely, but you need time to yourselves, there is another cottage on the property. The roof needs repairs, and we can buy some furniture, it'll be a great place to make a beginning."

I said, "Arigato Col. I will work hard to make it a home for Gerty. Can I use some of the money I have in the bank to buy a bed, mattress, and a table and chairs?"

The conversation was light, and as we were drinking, our conversation soon became incomprehensible. Eventually, Beth came in and chased us off to bed.

Early the next day Trevor and Col drove, Gerty and I to Greenvale.

The short informal service went off without any problems and soon we were signing the Registry and Marriage Certificate. I kissed my bride and Col took a photo of us. We were soon back in the truck, heading towards the homestead.

When we arrived home, we were pleasantly surprised to see that Beth had decorated the house with streamers and balloons. A great big sign over the entrance read,

"Welcome to Mr and Mrs Watanabe."

There was a beautiful wedding cake on a little table at the side, and the kitchen table was laid with a lovely white tablecloth and silver cutlery. Gerty and I felt greatly honoured.

As we walked in together, Col, Beth and Trevor clapped and cheered us. We couldn't have been happier.

Beth served up a wonderful meal and when we'd all finished, we moved to cut the cake together. Col took a photograph of us with his Brownie box camera.

Later, Gerty played some lovely tunes on the piano. Then Beth took over the piano so that Gerty and I could dance our Bridal Waltz to the tune of, 'The Loveliest Night of the Year.'

We had a wonderful celebration, and when we were finally alone, we promised each other to always be together and love each other for the rest of our lives.

I was the happiest I had ever been. We looked forward to a wonderful life together.

When we got time free from farm duties, Col, Trevor and I worked on the old farmhouse that was to become our future home.

Twelve months later, it had been transformed. We'd completely relined the inside and built in a new kitchen and pantry. Then we painted it throughout. Out the back Gerty had a chicken shed and a dozen chickens, water tanks, with flowing water connected to the kitchen and bathroom, and an iron bathtub. Trevor had purchased a queen-sized bed and mattress which Gerty, fitted out with a hand sewn doona and pillows. Beth had bought, sheets, towels and tablecloths, a toaster, and a Col had installed a wood burning stove. Col topped off our comfort by buying us a lounge and a lounge chair.

I had started with nothing. Here in Australia, the land I had sworn to attack, I had a beautiful home, a wonderful wife and a job that paid money.

I was grateful to Col, Beth and Trevor. Each Sunday we got together at Col's or our place where the ladies got the chance to show off their cooking skills. These were enjoyable social occasions where the men discussed farm business and the ladies discussed women's business.

On one Sunday night visit to our place Col brought us a special present.

We unwrapped it with great expectation. It was quite heavy. When we'd unwrapped it, we saw that it was a wireless radio.

I said to Col puzzled, "What can we plug it in to? We have no electricity."

Col, in his quiet Australian drawl answered, "Mate this is only half your gift. We've got a small generator on the back of the truck. We can put in some petrol, start it up, plug in the radio and turn it on."

Col and Trevor lifted the generator off the back truck and placed it onto the back veranda.

Col started it up and it started immediately and purred away quietly. Inside Trevor turned on the wireless. It crackled and popped incoherently. Col scratched his head for a while, snapped his fingers and then smiled as if a light had gone on in his brain.

"An aerial!" he said.

He went to his truck and came back with a length of thin copper wire, attached one end of the wire to the wireless and ran it up the wall and attached it to the architrave.

This time the voice was clear. The evening news was on.

"You beauty," said Trevor.

"You beauty," I echoed.

We all sat down and listened to the ABC broadcast. It was serious, eventful news,

"Reports are coming in from Germany that Adolf Hitler has committed suicide rather than allowing himself to be captured by the Russian troops invading Berlin. Although some German soldiers, old men and young boys are putting up resistance still trying to defend the capital, the War in Europe is effectively, over!"

All of us in the room felt a sense of relief.

"Attention now will turn to defeating the Japanese in the Pacific."

The War might soon be over against Japan," I told them.

"Would you like to go back to Japan?" "To go home?" asked Col.

I cuddled Gerty, smiled at her and said, "I am home Col. I don't want to go back there. I am an Aussie now and you are my family."

The wireless was a wonderful gift. Gerty and I sat on our comfortable lounge listening to our favourite music program. We loved listening to the music of Vera Lynn and Benny Goodman.

It was very relaxing sitting back, holding hands, tapping our feet to our favourite tunes in our own home.

One night as we were listening to the wireless the usual program was interrupted.

"We apologise to interrupt your program to bring you news that the United States has dropped an atomic bomb on the Japanese city of Hiroshima, killing over a hundred thousand people!"

I couldn't believe what I was hearing. I said to Gerty, "This is very bad, many innocent people have been killed."

Tears ran down my cheeks for my fellow Japanese. I was sobbing.

Gerty cuddled me, trying to calm me down. But it took a long time before I did.

A week later another bomb was dropped on the city of Nagasaki with similar effect. Japan, unable to match this kind of weapon, surrendered unconditionally. The War in the Pacific was over.

Col spoke to me one night soon after, "Dropping the A-Bombs might seem a harsh act, but it certainly stopped the War in the Pacific. Millions more soldiers fighting in Japan and the Pacific islands, Japanese and Allies, would have died if they allowed the War to continue. Consider it Shinzo. Japan started the War. The Allies were only fighting back."

"You are right Col. But I am sorry for 'my' people.' My people were burnt up'. They were not 'your' people that were burnt up. Innocent people who were going to work or school or the market."

I moped around for ages before I began to put it behind me and feel more like my old self. I threw myself into my work Gerty and I were happy together. Through this difficult time Gerty was a source of strength for me. This made me appreciate and love her even more than I had before.

In 1947 Gerty gave birth to our first child, little Tanya. Gerty had a good pregnancy and Beth assisted her with the delivery. She was a lovely little baby girl with big blue eyes like her mother. She had olive skin and black hair like me. I doted on her.

As she became a toddler, I took her on the front of the horse for slow rides around the home paddock. I enjoyed these rides as much as Tanya and we laughed together as we rode around.

By 1950, the War was behind us and the World was beginning to rebuild. We rarely mentioned it. By then I was venturing into Greenvale to get groceries and farming supplies. If anybody asked, Col told them that I was from China and no-one ever challenged him because there were other Chinese labourers in Greenvale.

If you paid in Aussie pounds in Greenvale, you could usually buy whatever you wanted.

Col had banked over nine hundred pounds into my account. We'd spent fifty pounds on our furniture, so I had eight hundred and fifty pounds remaining in the bank.

As we were walking down the main street, I noticed a sign in the Real Estate Agent's window. We stopped and Col read it for me.

It read, "For Sale – Halfway Service Centre and Roadhouse, halfway between Rockhampton and Greenvale – Five hundred pounds."

There was a coloured photograph of a service station with trees and rolling hills behind it. I thought it would be a perfect place for Gerty and I to build a future for our family.

"Can we go and take a look please Col?" I asked.

"Okay Mate. Thinking of buying it are you?" asked Col.

"Let's take a look first," I told him.

We left Greenvale and headed towards Rockhampton. It was a very long drive before we reached the Halfway Service Centre three hours later.

Our first view of it was impressing. It was in very good condition and was open. The proprietor kindly gave us a tour of the facilities. Everything was neat, clean and freshly painted. It was bonus, that tools and equipment were included in the price. The owner went over the sales figures and customer numbers. They looked very impressive.

Col, being a down to earth man, asked the proprietor why he was selling up.

"I don't mind you asking. It's the isolation. My wife wants us to go back to the city to live in Rockhampton to help care for her aging mother and father.

It's a profitable business. It brings in about five hundred pounds a month. It's perfectly situated being the only service station between Rocky and Greenvale," he said.

"What about the dining room?" asked Col.

"My wife, Thelma, runs that. Truckies and tourists need to eat. She cooks burgers, breakfast and makes great coffee," he told us, "It makes a good profit too."

"Well Shinzo what do you think?" asked Col.

"We talk in car Col," I answered.

We farewelled the proprietor and drove off.

"It looks pretty good to me, but the decision is up to you and Gerty."

"If you want it, I reckon you could offer him four hundred and fifty pounds, take it or leave it, and see what happens," he said.

When we got back to Greenvale a little bell clanged as they entered the estate agent's office.

"Did you take a look at the Service Centre?" he asked.

"Yes Sir," said Col, "and we're willing to offer four hundred and fifty pounds, today, if you sell it at our price," said Col.

"Look Mate. The price is fixed," he said.

"Well unfix it and you'll have four hundred and fifty pounds in your hand today. You'll earn quite a commission," said Col.

The estate agent rang the proprietor, "They'll pay four-hundred and fifty but not five hundred pounds today. What do you want me to tell them?"

"Sell it for four-hundred and fifty," echoed the agent. "Thank you, Bill, I'll phone you when the sale goes through."

"Well Mr Flanagan and Mr Watanabe, Mr Watson will accept four hundred and fifty pounds. I'll make up the papers for you," he said.

"Wait!" I said, "I must talk to my wife first. Can we phone her from here please?"

"Cetainly,' said the agent.

When Gerty answered the phone I said to her, "Gerty, we have the opportunity to buy a service station and restaurant. I have been out to see it and Col and I think it would be a bargain for us to make a life for the kids and ourselves. What do you think?"

"If you think it's good for the family then we should buy it. I'll back your judgement."

"Thank you," I said, "I'll see you when I get home. Bye."

"Sir, you have a deal," I said.

"We'll go up to the bank to get the money. Do you prefer cash or bank cheque?" asked Col.

"A bank cheque would be fine, thank you," said the agent.

"Gerty and I will be very happy at the Service Centre Col. What will you do with our house?" I asked.

"I don't know if you noticed but Trevor has been courting a lovely girl in Greenvale called Marlene Forster. I think they'll be getting married soon and they can move into your house," said Col.

"That's a good solution Col, they'll be happy there like we've been," I told him.

When we'd paid the four hundred and fifty pounds and I'd signed the deeds and conveyancing document, the agent told us that we could move into the Service Centre within four weeks, he'd phone when it became vacant.

We set off back to the homestead. I was excited. I had just bought a service station. Gerty would be so excited.

Beth and Gerty were thrilled when we broke the news.

The next three weeks were spent busily packing until finally we were ready to move to the Service Centre. Gerty and I decided to keep the existing name, 'The Halfway Service Centre' because the customers knew it by that name, and we wanted to keep them rolling through."

From the very start business was steady and the trucks were pulling in regularly to top up with diesel before they hit the 'outback.'

I had to order more fuel from Rockhampton because of the increasing demand.

Soon Gerty was bringing in a small fortune, cooking burgers, fried chips and making steaming hot coffee.

Little Tanya stood in her cot watching Mum and the steady stream of people coming into the restaurant. Occasionally, the truckies brought her felt toys with pound notes pinned on them. Everybody loved little Tanya.

By 1953 we had two more children, our boy Felix and another little girl we called Monnie. The three children looked like peas in a pod. When I could get away from the pumps, I chased them around the loungeroom and gave them rides on my back. These were happy, enjoyable family times that we all came to cherish.

Gerty would call out from the kitchen, "Shinzo be careful. They'll get hurt! I don't know who the children are and who are the adults in there."

"Not my kids. Look they're all cowboys and cowgirls," I'd call back.

We had a wonderful life at the Halfway Service Centre.

It was always busy. Until one day. A day that threatened to change everything, an official looking man dressed in a suit and tie, carrying a black briefcase came into the restaurant.

"Mr Watanabe," he enquired.

"Yes," I said.

"Mr Watanabe, I'm Mr Barton from the Department of Immigration. We have evidence that indicates you didn't come to Australia in a legal way. What have you got to say for yourself?" he asked.

"Mr Barton. I am Shinzo. I crashed here during the War back in 1942. I worked hard on a farm and saved up enough money to buy this Service Centre. I married Gerty, an Australian girl, and we have three children, Tanya, Felix and Monnie. We are so happy here. Why would you want to cause us trouble?" I asked.

"By the way how did you find out how I came to Australia and that I was Japanese?" I asked.

"We cross-referenced your name from your property registration, and we couldn't find your name on the births, deaths and marriages register. That's when we started looking for you here," he answered.

"Can we have a coffee and discuss this situation," said Barton.

A truckie came in and called to me, "Hey, G'day Shinzo! Hello Gerty! The usual please? I'll go and wash my hands," he said.

I sat down with Mr Barton and Gerty brought us two of her best hot coffees. Barton added sugar to his and stirred. He took a big sip and savoured it before swallowing. "Excellent," he said.

"Look Shinzo, I was sent out to bring you in. Shinzo the Japanese Pilot. I don't see any Japanese pilots here. I see a Service Centre Manager with a successful business and a lovely wife and children. I see before me an Australian businessman living with his wife and kids," said Barton.

Gerty came in and said, "It's very busy out here Shinzo. Can you please come and assist when you are able to?"

Barton said, "You go and help her serve. I'll go back and write my report and send you a letter after I report to my supervisors."

He drank down his coffee, got into his car and drove off. When Mr Barton had gone, I told Gerty the nature of his visit. She was upset and we weren't sure what we should do. She told me to phone Col and ask his advice.

When I got off the phone Gerty asked me what Col said.

"Col said 'Carry on as usual and wait for the letter,'" I told her.

We did as Col advised but we were both still very worried that this was going to spoil our happy life.

One windy morning early in September, the mail truck brought the letter that we'd been dreading. I opened it up and passed it to Gerty to read.

"Dear Mr and Mrs Watanabe. The manner in which Mr Watanabe entered Australia in 1942 is to be investigated. There will be a hearing in Rockhampton District Court on Monday the 15th of September. Please be in attendance. It would be in your best interest to seek legal representation to express your case."

We both felt sick in the stomach as our lives were unravelling before our very eyes.

"We should call Col, "I said to Gerty.

When Col got on the phone, Gerty read him the letter.

He said, "I'll contact my cousin, Abbott Marley, in Sydney. He's a very good young solicitor. I'll ask him to come up and speak for Shinzo. He will be our best hope," advised Col.

There were some very sad people at the Halfway Service Centre that night. Gerty put her arms around me and told me, "Whatever it takes, we will see it through together."

"Yes," I said, "But it might mean me being deported to Japan."

"Have faith in your solicitor. Col said he's very talented," said Gerty.

"He'll have to be to get me out of his one," I told her.

When the fifteenth arrived Col, Beth Gerty and I travelled to Rockhampton for the hearing. Fortunately, Abbott Marley had flown up from Sydney.

Thankfully Trevor and his fiancé Marlene agreed to look after the Service Centre and babysit the children for a few days. They were very kind to us.

Before we went into the courtroom Abbott Marley instructed me what I should and shouldn't say. He was a cordial gentleman with very colourful clothes. He wore white slacks, an orange shirt with a green tie and well-cut hounds tooth jacket. He had a pleasant manner of speaking. He shook hands with me and bowed in the Japanese custom. I bowed in response.

"Shinzo, Col has spoken to me at length on the telephone about your case. I am advising you not to say too much. Say nothing that they can hold against you. Sometimes they twist what you tell them," he advised.

Sure, answer their questions, but don't say too much. Don't waffle. Leave it to me to do most of the talking. We have a very good case for obtaining Citizenship. You are legally married to an Australian woman and you are the father of three Australian citizens. The Court would be committing a major moral error of judgement to try and deport you after all this time. You've got abundant evidence to prove you that are a good, hardworking person. You present as a model citizen"

"Sir. May I ask?" I said,

He said, "Yes?"

"What chance do we have of winning?" I asked.

"Good question. I'm not a betting man Shinzo but I believe we've got a better than eighty percent chance of winning today. Have faith in the law and put your trust in me. This is a case I am very interested in winning.

I nodded that I understood but I was visibly shaking. I was very nervous.

The magistrate entered and we all stood up to show respect. When there was silence, he began to speak.

"We are not here today to judge Mr Watanabe. We are here to decide if he is a suitable person to be accepted as an Australian citizen, or if he should be deported as an illegal alien," he began.

"I wish to invite Mr Barton, the representative from the Department of Immigration, to speak," he said.

"Your Honour, this is a complicated and unusual case. Mr Shinzo Watanabe admits that he first came to Australia during the War in a Japanese aircraft to drop bombs on Darwin. He dropped his bombs and subsequently was hit by Australian anti-aircraft flak. Although his plane was damaged and was slowly losing altitude, he managed to fly it into Northern Queensland. When the plane was about to crash, Mr Watanabe bailed out and was picked up by a farmer, Mr Trevor Flanagan. At that time, the farmers didn't turn him in to the authorities and instead, gave him work on their farm, fed him, and paid him for his labour.

As time went by, Mr Watanabe met and married an Australian girl, Gerty Williamson, and now the couple have three young children. With money he'd earned Mr and Mrs Watanabe purchased a Service Station, 'The Halfway Service Centre' halfway between Rockhampton and Greenvale. Their business is operating successfully.

The Department recommends that Mr Watanabe be either granted Australian Citizenship, or if the Court decides, be sent back to Japan," he concluded.

"We have an official from The National Truckdrivers Association, Mr Michael Pascoe to advocate for Mr Waranabe to stay," said the magistrate.

"You may speak Mr Pascoe."

"Thank you, your Honour. I have known the Watanabes since they took over the Halfway Service Centre some years ago. Shinzo and Gerty, are like an extended family to all the truckies. Shinzo has always ensured that he has plenty of fuel on hand and Gerty has fed us with good, wholesome food. The Halfway Service Centre has become our 'home away from home'. All the truckies love the children and bring them little gifts from time to time. Truckdrivers don't get home too often and having a well-cooked meal and seeing the children makes us feel a little less less homesick. If you deport Shinzo, there will be a lot of very sad truckies out there. On a personal note, I know one truckie who couldn't pay for his fuel because he hadn't received his payment yet.

Shinzo said, 'I can trust you Bert, pay me next time you come through.' Bert did pay of course.

In closing your Honour, let me say that I am relaying the feelings of more than six hundred truckies who have signed a petition to ask for Shinzo Watanabe to be allowed stay in Australia and continue operating the Halfway Service Centre."

Looking over his spectacles the magistrate said, "Thankyou Mr Pascoe. That is amazing."

"Looking at his papers, now I see that Mr. Watanabe has representation here in court. Would you please step forward Mr Abbott Marley."

"Your Honour. Before we send Mr Watanabe back to a homeland he doesn't wish to return to, let us consider which decision will do the 'most good', for all concerned. Consider, if we send him back his wife and children will probably be forced to go back with him as they are a legally married couple. In Japan, the marriage won't be recognised and Gerty, Tanya, Felix and Monnie will be regarded as, and treated, as aliens. Shinzo will be imprisoned as a deserter from the War.

So that answer leaves a family torn apart with the breadwinner sentenced to prison.

Imprisoning Shinzo here in Australia would deprive a young family of its Father and deprive Australia of an honest, hardworking citizen. The best outcome, I submit, is for Shinzo Watanabe to be granted Australian Citizenship and be left free to raise the young family he loves so dearly with his loving wife, Gerty, to keep providing service, and wonderful meals to six hundred or more truckies."

"Shinzo's bombs fell harmlessly into Darwin Harbour. He couldn't bear to kill anyone. Since he parachuted to earth, Shinzo has done nothing wrong. He has worked hard and even saved Trevor Flanagan's life when he was bitten by a large black snake. Shinzo Watanabe has been a good, kind natured man for over ten years in Australia. Your Honour, I believe that the best solution we can arrive at today is to grant this little battler, Citizenship," concluded Abbott Marley.

The magistrate called Abbott Marley and the Immigration Official closer for a conference.

He asked the Immigration Official, "Do you think Marley's proposal is acceptable?"

He replied, "Yes your Honour. I don't want to send this little bloke back to Japan."

"Nor do I," said the magistrate, "That's it then. We'll let him remain in Australia and grant him Citizenship.

"This is an acceptable outcome your Honour," said Marley.

Just then they heard a loud 'blast' from a truck horn. Then another loud truck horn blast, then another until the air was filled with a cacophony of truck horns all sounding simultaneously. The noise was deafening.

"Sheriff!" called the magistrate, "Go out and see what's going on, and quieten them down. We're not finished here yet!"

He came back in a few minutes later and reported to the magistrate.

"There's about three hundred big rigs out there that have come to ask for Shinzo to stay. They've all got signs and they're chanting, 'Let him stay! Let him stay!' he said.

"Go out onto the steps and hold up your thumb to signal 'Yes'. That might quieten them down," said the magistrate.

He did so but it didn't silence them. There was a tremendous roar of approval when they received the news. They were cheering and clapping and honking their horns. Finally, sanity prevailed, and they quietened down. They'd all been happy to come to Rockhampton to show their support for Shinzo and his family.

"The Court had decided," he announced. "Shinzo Watanabe came to this land as an enemy. He had sworn to kill as many Australians as he could.

But Mr Watanabe had never met an Australian. When Col Flanagan, Trevor and Beth showed him the kindness that only good people can show, Shinzo changed.

He worked hard and gradually came to be one of the Flanagan clan. Shinzo came to love the people around him and the land upon which he toiled.

He doesn't want to go back to Japan. He wants to remain in Australia and raise his family.

The Court believes that he would make a better Service Centre Manager than a Japanese prisoner. Therefore, we have decided that Shinzo Watanabe will be granted Australian Citizenship. What do you say Mr Watanabe?"

There was clapping and cheering in the court. I rose to speak.

"Your Honour. I am very pleased with the court's decision. I would never do anything to hurt Australia or Australian people. It is my home. Thank you, Sir," I said.

We celebrated at the Rockhampton Bowling Club. I was so happy I thought my heart would burst. I hugged Gerty. We had a lovely lunch and we were all in a buoyant mood. Champagne corks were popping, and everyone was celebrating. Mike Pascoe came over to wish us well and there were lots of other truckies in for lunch and they kept coming up and shaking my hand saying, "Well done Shinzo."

"I can't wait to tell Trevor and Marlene the good news," I said.

"Why don't you phone them. There's a phone in the foyer," said Col.

Gerty and I hurried off to use the phone.

Col turned to his cousin Abbott Marley and spoke quietly, "You were brilliant in there today Abbott. I can see that your experience in Sydney has really developed your legal skills, how much do we owe you for today?"

"Thanks Col but I'm doing this one 'pro bono,' for you," he said.

'What's that mean Abbott?" asked Col.

"Latin Dear Chap. Translated it means, I'm giving my services for free," said Marley.

"Are you sure. Can we pay your expenses?" Col asked.

"No Col. It was my absolute pleasure to see Shinzo granted Citizenship. Don't forget, we are family. I am happy to come here and see you and Beth again," he said,

"I must go now. I'm flying out of Rockhampton at six o'clock."

He shook hands with them all and walked out to catch his taxi. I caught him just in time and thanked him for helping us, "Arigato," I said.

He replied, "My pleasure Shinzo."

After the hearing life went very well for us.

The trucks kept rolling in and the children were growing bigger every day. Over time I got the opportunity to thank them all for turning up at the Rockhampton courthouse and supporting me.

I told Gerty that we deserved some time away from the Service Centre as a family and that we could afford to hire a couple to work while we went away. So were placed an advertisement in the Rockhampton Gazette and a lovely newly married couple replied. Jenny and David Cooper were their names. We employed them both and eventually after they'd spent six months in a caravan, we built a little cottage on the land behind the Service Centre for them.

Gerty taught Jenny to run the restaurant and I taught David how to run the fuel pumps. They were both interested in learning. They loved our kids and they became part of our extended family. We could trust David and Jenny with the running of all aspects the Service Centre.

In 1955 I took Gerty and the kids for a holiday down in Brisbane. We stayed at the Gold Coast and we all loved it. For the first time in my life ventured into the surf. I noticed a man riding the waves on a surfboard. He paddled to get the board moving and then stood up and rode the wave. I watched for a while and thought to myself, "I can do that."

So, I hired a surfboard and carried it to the waters' edge and paddled out to where the other riders were waiting. When the waves came, I paddled for my life. When I felt the wave pushing me forward, I put my hands on the sides of the board and eased myself up as I'd seen the other surfers do. I was standing up. I felt excited as the water foamed around my feet, when suddenly I was flying over the front of the board as the nose dug in. I went under the water and as I came up the following wave hit me in the face. I turned and swam after the board and kept trying. After a few hours, I was beginning to manage it.

The next day we visited Frank Evans' Porpoise Pool and Aquarium at Tweed Heads. It featured an amazing display of aquatic animals. Felix was particularly excited to watch a young lady in a bikini stand up on a platform and hold out a little fish. A dolphin came jumping up and took the fish from the lady's hand. Felix clapped and cheered as the big dolphin splashed back into down into the water.

I particularly enjoyed the vintage automobiles on display at Gilltrap's Automobile Museum at Currumbin. Engines have always fascinated me, so I enjoyed the sounds, smells and styles of the wonderful old cars as they puttered around the viewing area. Gerty, the kids and I had a ride in a famous old car called 'Genevieve' which was to be used in a movie.

Each night the family had a barbecue at the house where we were staying. Gerty and I celebrated the Court decision that allowed us to remain together.

We enjoyed leisurely walks down the white sandy beaches in the evenings and watched the stars coming out and shining on the water. The children paddled and jumped in the water and felt the gentle waves wash over their feet. Gerty and I made sandcastles with them on the beach and had a lovely time playing together.

We all enjoyed the holiday and vowed to take time out each year to return to this enchanting place.

After our two glorious weeks on the Gold Coast, we boarded the small TAA passenger plane and flew back to Rockhampton. Col and Beth were there to meet us at the airport. It was a wonderful homecoming.

On the way back to the Halfway Service Centre we were all talking at once. Col couldn't believe his ears when I described riding the waves on a surfboard. Little Felix described the jumping dolphins and made us all laugh, "He jump up and eat the little fishy, Uncle Col," he said excitedly.

We were all glad to come home and pleased with the way David and Jenny had looked after the place. Trevor turned to Col and said, "We have a surprise for you!" said Trevor, "Marlene is expecting!"

We all smiled and congratulated them. Marlene was glowing.

The following Sunday we all had a big dinner together at Col's house. David and Jenny looked after the Service Centre while we drove over to Col's. When we'd all finished our meal, Col gave a speech,

"Fate moves us in different ways. Our Shinzo flew here to attempt to kill us. He was at war. But now Shinzo is one of our family. Shinzo, Gerty and their children, Tanya, Felix and Monnie, Trevor and Marlene and their baby are all one big happy family. Shinzo and Gerty have a profitable business and Trevor and Marlene have a profitable farm with many cattle and sheep. We all have lot to be thankful for." We all clapped when Col was finished.

I stood up and said, "I would like to say a few words!"

"There are two people, who have made all this possible. We owe them a great deal of thanks. Raise your glasses and drink a toast to Col and Beth," I said.

They did so, "To Col and Beth."

"To Col and Beth!" they all echoed.

We all drank the toast.

The tourists looked at each other.

"Shinzo, that was a wonderful story. Thank you for relating it to us. But now we must get into our Winnebago and head West again," said Peter.

They paid for their food and fuel and climbed into the vehicle. Their children followed them and jumped in.

Gerty and I waved farewell. Just as he was about to drive away, he stopped and called out, "Hey Shinzo!"

I went over to him and he said, "'Arigato, Shinzo my friend," shaking my hand.

I said back to him, "Arigato to you Peter and Jennifer, have a safe and enjoyable journey,"

As they drove away, dust rose and hung in the air for a while. Soon they were swallowed up by the ranges.

Gerty and I took the children inside to give them their dinner. It had been another interesting day. "Come to think of it," I thought to myself, "So far, I've had an interesting life."

....